B is for
Baby

Atinuke

Angela Brooksbank

WALKER BOOKS
AND SUBSIDIARIES
LONDON · BOSTON · SYDNEY · AUCKLAND

For Adia, with love! ~ A.

For my father also known as Baba, who took me to Africa when I was a Baby. ~ A.B.

First published 2019 by Walker Books Ltd, 87 Vauxhall Walk, London SE11 5HJ

Text © 2019 Atinuke ✪ Illustrations © 2019 Angela Brooksbank

The right of Atinuke and Angela Brooksbank to be identified as the author and illustrator respectively of this work
has been asserted by them in accordance with the Copyright, Designs and Patents Act 1988

British Library Cataloguing in Publication Data: a catalogue record for this book is available from the British Library ✪ ISBN 978-1-4063-7108-6 ✪ www.walker.co.uk ✪ 10 9 8 7 6 5 4 3 2 1

B is for

Baby.

B is for Beads.

B is for Basket.

B is for **Banana.**

B is for **Breakfast.**

B is for Brother.

B is for going
to see **Baba.**

B is for **Bicycle.**

B is for **Bumpy.**

B is for **Baobab.**

B is for **Big.**

B is for **Butterfly**.
B is for **Bird**.

B is for **Beautiful.**

B is for **Baboon.**

B is for **Bus.**

B is for Bridge.

B is for
Bougainvillea.

B is for
Bungalow.

B is for ... Baba!

B is for ...
Bananas?

B is for ...
Baby!

B is for **Biscuit!**

B is for Biscuit, Bananas and Baba.

B is for Baboon,

B is for Bicycle, Brother and Basket. And...

Bungalow, Bridge and Bus.

Butterfly and Bird.

B is for
Baby.